540L ✐ W9-BUS-316

THE BUBBLE FACTORY™

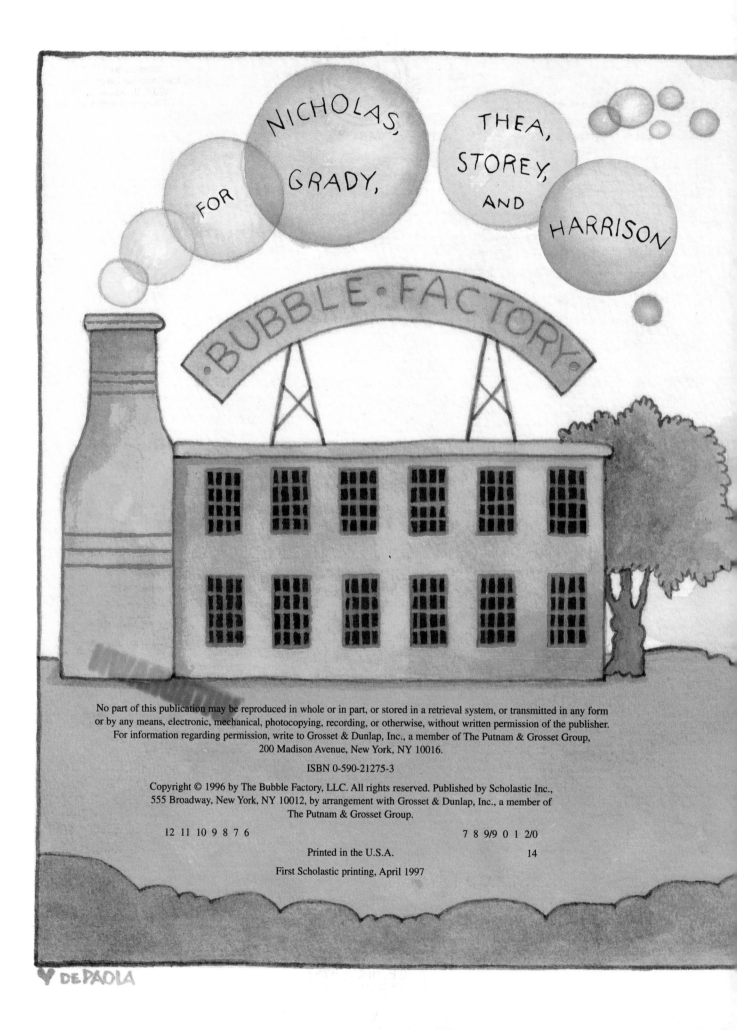

FOR NICHOLAS, GRADY, THEA, STOREY, AND HARRISON

BUBBLE • FACTORY

ISBN 0-590-21275-3

Copyright © 1996 by The Bubble Factory, LLC. All rights reserved. Published by Scholastic Inc., 555 Broadway, New York, NY 10012, by arrangement with Grosset & Dunlap, Inc., a member of The Putnam & Grosset Group.

12 11 10 9 8 7 6   7 8 9/9 0 1 2/0

Printed in the U.S.A.   14

First Scholastic printing, April 1997

dePAOLA

THE BUBBLE FACTORY

Tomie dePaola

SCHOLASTIC INC.
New York Toronto London Auckland Sydney

Sam and Molly were always getting into things…

and Grampa was always getting them out.

So one day he handed the twins jars of bubbles to keep them out of trouble. Double Bubbles, they were called, because with each wave of the double wand, out came not one, but TWO bubbles.

"Perfect for twins," Grampa said, "and made right here
in town at the Bubble Factory where I used to work."
"The Bubble Factory!" the twins said at the same time.
"Would you take us there today?"

So off they went. Before long they turned down a winding road. And there it was. It looked like any ordinary factory. Except for what was coming out of the chimney. Bubbles! Lots and lots of bouncy bubbles in every color you can imagine! Sam and Molly couldn't wait to go inside.

Grampa introduced them to Mr. B., the Head Bubblemaker,
who was just as round as a bubble himself.

"I'm going to show you exactly how bubbles are made,"
Mr. B. told the twins.

The first stop was the great Bubble Machine, a maze of
wheels and gears and levers and pulleys.

Jar after jar popped onto a belt. Mechanical arms moved up and down placing a wand in each one, then filling and capping them.

Next they visited the Bubble Bathery. Here, new kinds
of bubble bath were being tested in big bathtubs by a
Bubble-O-Meter.

Down the hall was a Bubble Boutique with really fancy
bubbles floating everywhere—polka-dotted ones, striped
ones, even bubbles with your name on them.

In the Bubble Gummery next door, brand-new bubble gum
was being invented—whistling bubble gum, non-popping
bubble gum, and bubble gum that did the chewing for you.
Mechanical heads were test-blowing bubbles—one had pink
goo all over its metal face.

The last stop was the Bubble Lab. This was the place where the bubbles of the future were invented—bubbles which had started out as only an idea in someone's head.

"Can we see them?" the twins asked.

Mr. B. shook his head. "Sorry, but it's too soon. They're not ready yet."

Just then a Bubble Worker came to get Mr. B. "Mr. B., you're expected at the 11 o'clock Bubble Board Meeting."

"Come with me," Mr. B. said to Grampa. "Everyone will want to see you."

Grampa looked at the twins. "If I go, will you two stay out of trouble?" The twins nodded. So Mr. B. led them out into the hallway and sat them on a bubble bench.

"Stay right here until I get back," Grampa told them. "I won't be long."

Sam and Molly meant to do exactly what Grampa said.
But Mr. B. had left the door to the Bubble Lab open!

So, quicker than it takes a bubble to pop, they were inside again. Sam took one jar. Molly took another. They looked at each other. "Let's try them!" they said together, and went back to the Bubble Machine.

All the Bubble Workers were at the meeting. The Bubble Machine was turned off. "I see the ON button," Sam said. They both reached for it and pushed. The machine gave a giant BLUB! "Now what do we do?" Sam asked.

Molly pointed to a large funnel with a sign on it that said POUR HERE.

So they did—a little from Sam's Jar A and a little from Molly's Jar B. At first nothing happened.

But Sam and Molly kept hoping. Then suddenly, bubbles by the billions came whooshing out of the machine!

"Look what's happening to the bubbles," said Molly.
"Wow!" said Sam. "It's all of our wishes come true."

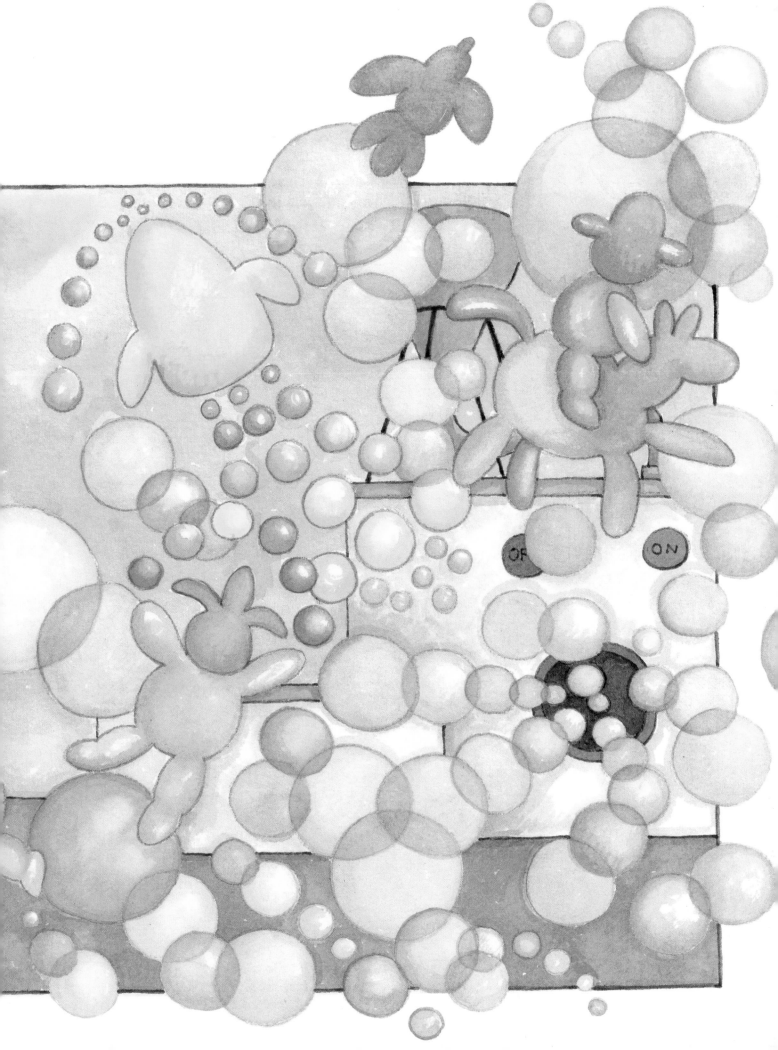

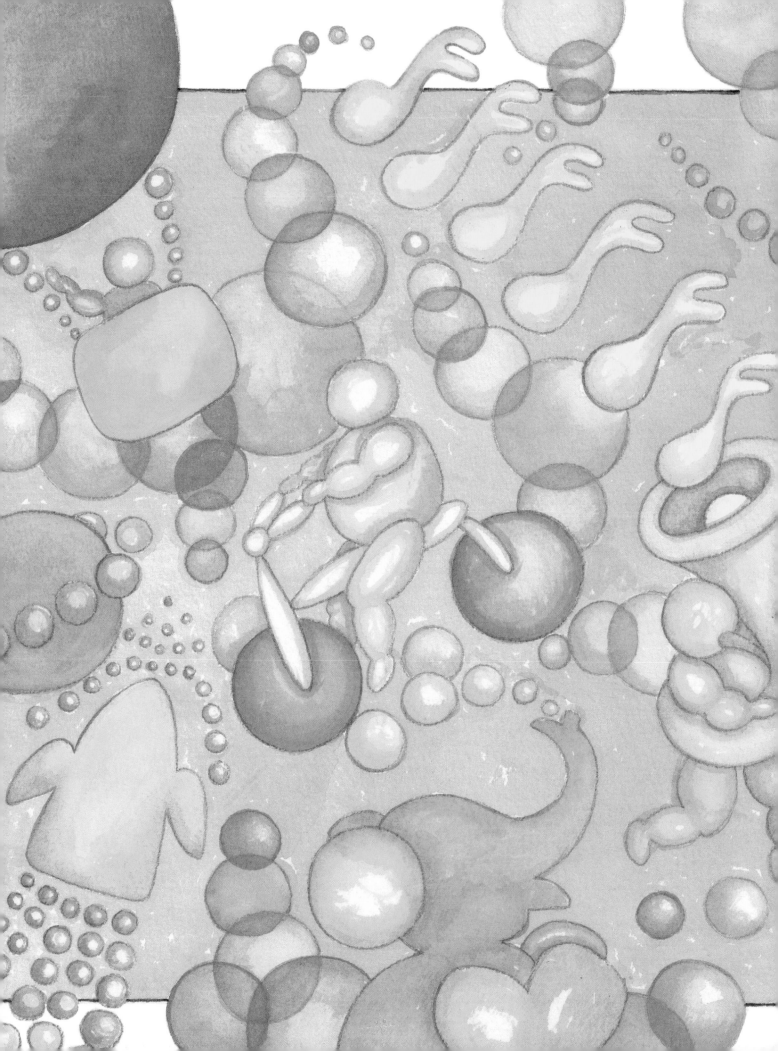

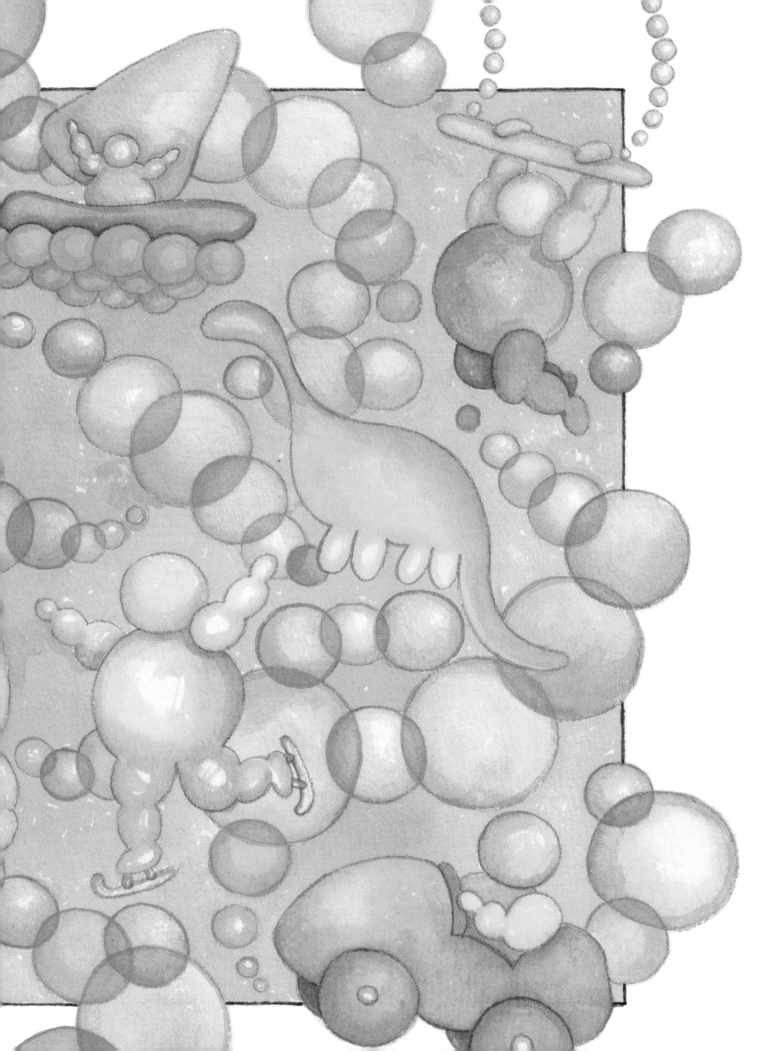

The twins could not believe their eyes. "What did we do?" Molly asked.

"I don't know. But let's do it again!" Sam said.

They were just about to pour in more from Jar A and Jar B when Grampa and Mr. B. came running in.

"What's going on here!" Mr. B. asked. "We just saw a
bubble rocket coming out of the chimney!"

Sam and Molly looked at each other. "I'm sorry," Molly
said. "We didn't mean to make such a mess."

Sam nodded. "I wish there were some way for us to clean
it up."

No sooner said than done!

Out of the Bubble Machine came a clean-up squad of vacuum cleaners, brooms, dustpans, and mops. They all went to work.

In a flash everything was back as it had been before.
Grampa and Mr. B. stood with their mouths open.

"This is amazing," cried Mr. B. "No one has ever made
bubbles like this before! What did you do?"

Sam and Molly showed Mr. B. the bottles. "It's easy. All you do is put in some of Jar A and some of Jar B. Then your wishes come true."

"You've made WISH BUBBLES!" said Grampa.
"We've been trying to do that for years!" said Mr. B.
"We need you around here. Will you come back? Who
knows what else you'll dream up!"

That was fine with Sam and Molly. When it was time to
leave, they got a big send-off...

and a ride home in Mr. B.'s Bubble Mobile.

That night after Grampa kissed them each goodnight, they felt something under their pillows.

Bubble jars with a note from Mr. B.